# CARTER AND CHLOE TWIN Adventures

WRITTEN BY: ZENOBIA MOORE

WITH: HEDDRICK MCBRIDE

ILLUSTRATED BY: HH-PAX

# DEDICATION

This book is dedicated to my loving husband, Jason Moore, and our wonderful twins, Carter and Chloe Moore.

Jason, thank you for being my unwavering support, for turning my dreams into reality, and for teaching me the true meaning of love. You have given me the greatest gift of all—our beautiful twins.

Carter, your bright eyes and adventurous spirit show me that you are destined to make a powerful impact on this world. I cannot wait to see how God uses your artistic talents to bless the world. You will always be my favorite superhero, with your signature white socks and black sneakers.

Chloe, your sweet soul and wisdom beyond your years are a constant reminder that God blessed this world the moment you arrived. My little love bug, you'll always be my favorite dancer, especially when the music plays in the car.

I am endlessly grateful to have the three of you in my life. I will always love you, #241—*Too Much, Forever, and Once "Moore."*

To my parents, Zenobia Carter Moultrie and the late Clinton Moultrie: Thank you for always being the wind beneath my wings.

# STORY 1: THE MOORE FAMILY FUN DAY AT THE PARK

Carter and Chloe raced down the sidewalk, their hands swinging back and forth. "Slow down, slow down!" their mommy called, laughing as she struggled to keep up. The twins giggled in unison, their excitement bubbling over. They had arrived at the park! Chloe tugged on her mom's sleeve. "Mommy, up! Mommy, pick me up!" Carter, full of energy, raced ahead to the jungle gym. "Watch this, Chloe!" he shouted, already showing off as he swung across the monkey bars.

Once Chloe reached the top of the jungle gym, she spotted the tall slide. "Weee!" she yelled as she zoomed down, her laughter filling the park. Carter, not to be outdone, stood at the base of the tallest slide and puffed out his chest. "I'm going up!" he announced with a grin. He climbed up and slid down faster than ever. "Whoosh! Beat that!" he said.

Chloe replied, "I'll race you to the swings!"

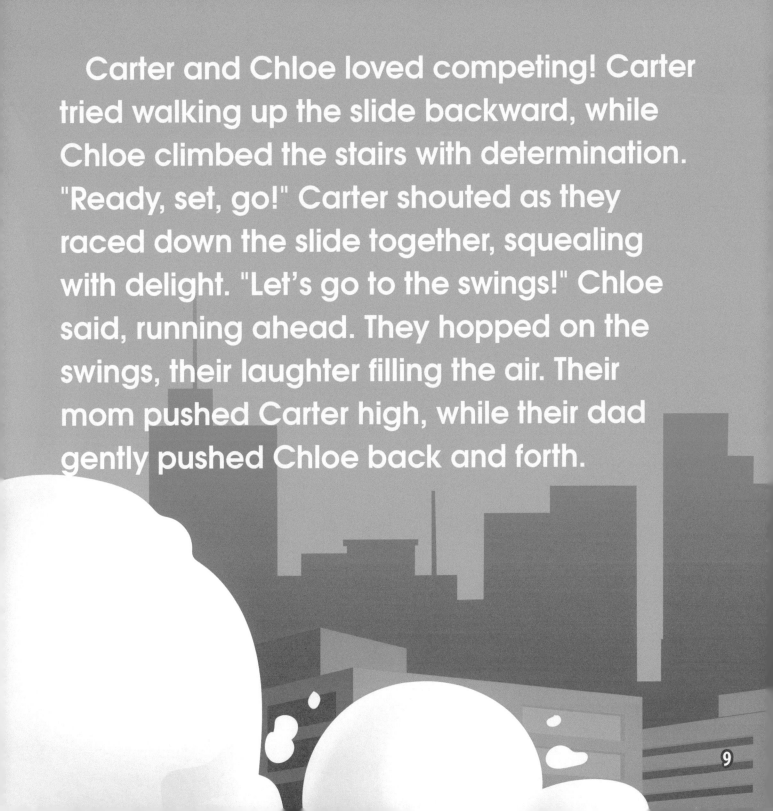

Carter and Chloe loved competing! Carter tried walking up the slide backward, while Chloe climbed the stairs with determination. "Ready, set, go!" Carter shouted as they raced down the slide together, squealing with delight. "Let's go to the swings!" Chloe said, running ahead. They hopped on the swings, their laughter filling the air. Their mom pushed Carter high, while their dad gently pushed Chloe back and forth.

After the swings, the twins ran to the sandbox to build a castle. Carter dug deep tunnels, while Chloe found flowers to decorate the top. "Look at this, Carter!" Chloe said, adding a flower on top of her tower. "We're building a castle for a queen and king!" Carter added some water to his tunnels and said, "It's a royal fortress!"

Next, they skipped to the see-saw. "I'm a superhero!" Carter shouted, raising his arm like he was flying. Chloe balanced herself on the opposite end, laughing. "I'm a princess superhero!" she said, imitating her brother. The see-saw bounced up and down, with their dad helping push Carter higher, while their mom balanced Chloe's side. "Look at me, I'm flying!" Carter yelled.

Chloe responded, "Superheroes can save the day together!"

Just before it was time to go home, Carter and Chloe spotted a family of ducks near the pond. "Look, baby ducks!" Chloe squealed. Their dad handed them a bag of breadcrumbs. "Feed them, but gently!" Carter threw a piece of bread, and the ducklings quacked loudly in thanks. Chloe knelt down, letting the tiny ducks nibble from her hand. "I love ducks!" she said, smiling brightly.

Now that playtime was over, the Moore Family grabbed hands and began to walk home. "Wait! Let's take a picture for Instagram," their dad said, pulling out his phone. "Say cheese!" Carter and Chloe made funny faces while their mom and dad laughed. "Hashtag #MooreFamilyFunDay," their dad said with a wink.

# STORY 2: TAKING CARE OF MY TWIN. I GOT YOUR BACK, BRO!

Chloe was always there to help her twin brother, Carter, every single day. On Monday, Carter stood at the top of the stairs, hesitating. "It's too high!" he said nervously. Chloe took his hand and grinned. "Don't worry, I've got you!" Together, they jumped, their feet landing safely on the ground. "See? Easy!" Chloe said, proud of their jump.

On Tuesday, Carter spilled bubbles all over the bathroom floor. He was put in time-out, but Chloe wouldn't leave his side. "I'll wait with you, Carter," she whispered. Together, they sat quietly until Carter was free. "Thanks, Chloe," Carter said. On Wednesday, when Carter didn't want to eat his peas, Chloe had an idea. "Let's hide them!" she giggled, sneaking peas under her knees. Carter laughed so hard, he almost forgot he didn't like peas.

On Thursday, the loud hum of the vacuum cleaner scared Carter. He covered his ears and backed away quickly. "Come here, Carter!" Chloe called, grabbing his hand. She led him to the stairs, and they sat together until the noise stopped. "See, it's not so bad," she whispered, giving him a hug. Carter sighed in relief. "Thanks, Chloe."

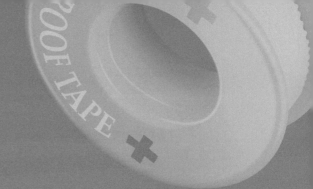

On Sunday, the family was dancing around the living room. "Spin, spin, spin!" Carter cheered. But he tripped and scraped his knee. Chloe rushed over. "I'll get a band-aid!" she said. Moments later, Carter was all patched up, and they were back to dancing.

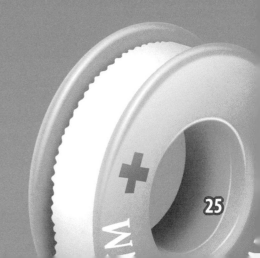

# STORY 3: TWIN DREAMING

Chloe and Carter said their nightly prayers and echoed their mother softly whispering, "I love you too much, forever, and once more." Their mother quietly walked out the door as the twins closed their eyes and dozed off to sleep. Chloe turned to her right and began dreaming of dancing with her father at a grand ball, twirling around and around as if the night would never end. The music played in her head, and she felt like a princess. Meanwhile, Carter turned to his right, dreaming of being a brave ninja, showing off his cool moves to his friends. He jumped, flipped, and kicked, feeling like the strongest ninja in the world.

# About the Author

Zenobia Moore, a native of New Castle, Delaware, has dedicated much of her professional and personal life to serving the Maryland community. She is a proud first-generation graduate of Morgan State University, where she earned a Bachelor's degree in Social Work with a minor in Criminal Justice. During her time at Morgan, she became a proud member of Alpha Kappa Alpha Sorority, Incorporated. Zenobia later continued her education at the University of Maryland School of Social Work, earning a Master's degree in Social Work.

With over two decades of experience, Zenobia has combined her personal passion and professional expertise to help others through the field of Social Work. Recently, she expanded her impact as an adjunct professor at the Graduate School of Social Work at Morgan State University, where she is committed to mentoring and guiding the next generation of Urban Social Workers.

Although she has achieved many professional accomplishments, Zenobia considers her most important role to be that of a wife and mother. She lives by the motto, "*The load of life may be heavy, but it is liftable,*" embodying her dedication to uplifting and supporting others.

# VISIT
## www.mcbridestories.com

# " Moore" moments that inspired the author